1853

Cécile's GIFT

By DENISE LEWIS PATRICK

ILLUSTRATIONS CHRISTINE KORNACKI

VIGNETTES CINDY SALANS ROSENHEIM

★ American Girl®

THE AMERICAN GIRLS

1764

KAYA, an adventurous Nez Perce girl whose deep love for horses and respect for nature nourish her spirit

1774

FELICITY, a spunky, spritely colonial girl, full of energy and independence

1824

JOSEFINA, a Hispanic girl whose heart and hopes are as big as the New Mexico sky

1853

CÉCILE AND MARIE-GRACE, two girls whose friendship helps them—and New Orleans—survive terrible times

1854

KIRSTEN, a pioneer girl of strength and spirit who settles on the frontier

1864 ADDY, a courageous girl determined to be free in the midst of the Civil War

1904 SAMANTHA, a bright Victorian beauty, an orphan raised by her wealthy grandmother

1914 REBECCA, a lively girl with dramatic flair growing up in New York City

1934 KIT, a clever, resourceful girl facing the Great Depression with spirit and determination

1944 MOLLY, who schemes and dreams on the home front during World War Two

1974 JULIE, a fun-loving girl from San Francisco who faces big changes—and creates a few of her own

Published by American Girl Publishing, Inc.
Copyright © 2011 by American Girl, LLC

Questions or comments? Call 1-800-845-0005, visit **americangirl.com**, or write to Customer Service, American Girl, 8400 Fairway Place, Middleton, WI 53562-0497.

Printed in China
11 12 13 14 15 16 LEO 10 9 8 7 6 5 4 3 2 1

Profound appreciation to Mary Niall Mitchell, Associate Professor of History, University of New Orleans; Sally Kittredge Reeves, former Notarial Archivist, New Orleans; and Thomas A. Klingler, Associate Professor, Department of French and Italian, Tulane University

PICTURE CREDITS
The following individuals and organizations have generously given permission to reprint images contained in "Looking Back":
p. 75—Courtesy of Shelley Cornia; pp. 76–77—Wisconsin Historical Society, Whi-78209 (people donating money); © Bettmann/Corbis (shipment of supplies); © Bettmann/Corbis, detail (nun visiting the sick); Sisters of the Holy Family Archives (Henriette Delille); pp. 78–79—Picture Collection, The New York Public Library, Astor, Lenox and Tilden Foundations, detail (benefit concert); Picture History (child actors); pp. 80–81—Music Division, The New York Public Library for the Performing Arts, Astor, Lenox and Tilden Foundations (Jenny Lind); Eno Collection, Miriam and Ira D. Wallach Division of Art, Prints and Photographs, The New York Public Library, Astor, Lenox and Tilden Foundations (ticket stub); Courtesy of Jackie Napolean Wilson (quartet of musicians); The Historic New Orleans Collection, accession no. 92-48-L Mss 536, Armstrong, f. 320; pp. 82–83—© iStockphoto/ JohnPeacock (jambalaya); Courtesy of Artisan Style Photojournalism (marching band); Kordcom Kordcom/Photolibrary (Bourbon Street); © iStockphoto/vernonrd (St. Louis Cathedral).

Cataloging-in-Publication data available from the Library of Congress

FOR YOU, NEW ORLEANS

Cécile and her family speak both English and French, just as many people from New Orleans did. You'll see some French words in this book. For help in pronouncing or understanding the foreign words, look in the glossary on page 83.

Table of Contents

Cécile's Family and Friends

CÉCILE'S FAMILY

PAPA
Cécile's father, a warm, gentle man and a successful sculptor

MAMAN
Cécile's mother, who is firm but kind and is a good businesswoman

CÉCILE
A confident, curious girl who loves the limelight

ARMAND
Cécile's older brother, who has been studying in Paris, France

GRAND-PÈRE
Cécile's loving grandfather, a retired sailor with many tales to tell

TANTE OCTAVIA AND RENÉ
Maman's widowed sister and her son, who live with Cécile's family

MADAME OCÉANE
Marie-Grace's aunt, a young opera singer

MARIE-GRACE
Cécile's friend, who moved back to New Orleans after several years away

MATHILDE
The Reys' housekeeper and cook

PERRINE DUPREE
A girl who is staying at Children of Mercy Orphanage

CHAPTER ONE

GREAT THINGS

October 1853

Cécile stood for a moment in the sunlight on her way to Holy Trinity Orphanage and glanced up at the beautiful blue sky. The few fluffy white clouds scampered quickly away, as if nothing could stand in the way of a clear and perfect day.

Her brother, Armand, had just waved a jaunty good-bye and gone on his way to do some sketching in Jackson Square. Cécile watched his thin figure until he turned out of sight. She felt amazed and grateful that he had recovered so well from his terrible illness of the summer. Many people had not been so fortunate. Cécile thought sadly of her family's maid, Ellen, who had died of yellow fever—just like thousands of other people across New Orleans.

Cécile began walking again, drinking in the ordinary sounds of people chatting outside shops, horses trotting and wagons rumbling, and *marchandes* calling on street corners to sell their snacks and trinkets. During the worst of the epidemic, Cécile remembered, the city had grown still and silent, because anyone who was not sick was caring for those who were. She looked up at the clear October sky and whispered a prayer of thanks that New Orleans was finally coming back to life. She hoped it would soon sound just as lively and bustling as it used to.

And then, as she started up the steps to Holy Trinity Orphanage, she added another prayer— a prayer for the many children who had lost their parents during this terrible summer. Holy Trinity was one of the places where the children were being cared for, and Cécile was here to help. She pushed open the door and stepped into the sunny hallway.

"Cécile! There you are," her friend Marie-Grace called from the top of the staircase.

"*Bonjour*, Marie-Grace!" Cécile waved.

"Sister Beatrice has given us a job to do," Marie-Grace said. Sister Beatrice was the director of Holy Trinity and a good friend of Cécile's *maman.* "But first, I have news!"

Cécile tugged off her coat and hat and hurried up the stairs. "Whatever is it?" she asked. She could see that Marie-Grace wasn't just smiling. She was beaming. Cécile could feel her excitement.

Marie-Grace clasped her arm. "Uncle Luc and Aunt Océane have decided to take a wedding trip!"

Cécile smiled, recalling the wedding of Marie-Grace's uncle and the girls' dear voice teacher right here in the chapel of Holy Trinity. The wedding had been small but *magnifique,* with flowers that she and Marie-Grace had arranged and a beautiful hymn sung by Marie-Grace.

"They're going to Belle Chênière," Marie-Grace continued, "and I'm going to go with them! Papa says I might stay two or three months!"

"That's wonderful!" Cécile hugged her friend. Ever since Marie-Grace and her father had moved back to New Orleans in January, she had wanted to visit the village where her mother grew up. Cécile knew that Marie-Grace had many cousins there, and she had not seen them for several years.

"We're leaving in a month," Marie-Grace added, "and I'll be busy helping Aunt Océane get ready for the trip." Cécile heard the love in her voice as she said the words *Aunt Océane*.

"I'll miss you, but I'm so happy for you," Cécile said, and she meant it from her heart.

"I'll write to you," Marie-Grace said. "And you'll have to write back!"

"Perhaps," Cécile teased, laughing because Marie-Grace knew that she didn't like writing very much. "Now, we'd better get to work. What does Sister Beatrice need us to do?"

"Three more children arrived today, and Sister Beatrice wants us to find places for them to sleep."

The girls started down the hall, making their way around baskets piled with donated toys, neatly folded clothing, and clean linens. They glanced into rooms already crowded with narrow beds.

"*C'est impossible!*" exclaimed Cécile. "There's no space left."

"Let's look in the music room," Marie-Grace suggested.

The girls hurried farther down the hall and stepped into the large room. It was filled with child-sized cots. "Where's the piano?" Cécile asked. Then she saw that it had been pushed into a corner to make space for baby cribs. Signs of little children littered the floor—here was a tiny handkerchief; there was a rag doll. Cécile spied a slingshot on the floor and bent to pick it up. "Armand used to have one of these," she said gently, wondering which of the children outside owned this prize.

Marie-Grace didn't respond. She walked to the window and looked down into the courtyard, where dozens of children were lining up for their morning treat. Cécile joined her. They watched as nuns passed out one small orange for each hungry stomach. Some children chatted with one another while they ate; others sat alone.

Cécile thought of her own family gathered around the dinner table, sharing stories and laughter as they ate together. "The children must miss their parents terribly," she said. She touched Marie-Grace's shoulder. "Will you miss your maman forever?"

Marie-Grace nodded. "I can't imagine what I would have done if I'd lost Papa, too," she said softly.

Cécile suddenly sat down on the nearest bed. She laid one hand gently on the thin blanket and thought of Maman tucking her into her soft, cozy bed each night. Her throat felt tight. How could anything make up for what the children had lost?

"Do you think we're *really* helping the orphans, Marie-Grace?" she asked.

Marie-Grace turned to face her. "Of course we are," she said firmly. "We make beds and peel potatoes for supper. And we spend time with the children. Why, only *you* can get the little ones to sit still. When you tell one of your stories or recite a rhyme, your make-believe seems so real! You help them forget their troubles for a while."

"And the children always want you to make up games for them," Cécile added. She smiled and stood up. "I guess you're right. But I wish I could do magic now. *Poof!*" She snapped her fingers. "I would make beds appear like so!"

Marie-Grace laughed, and Cécile was happy that they had cheered each other.

Just then, the girls heard the screeching of

carriage wheels outside, and then loud voices in the entrance hall. They rushed to the landing and leaned over the banister. Cécile saw the orphanage doors thrown open and several nuns hurrying outside.

"What's happening?" Marie-Grace asked.

Cécile marched downstairs to find out. With Marie-Grace at her heels, she hurried through the entrance hall and peered out the door.

A delivery wagon was stopped at a wild angle across the street, and the driver was trying to calm his horses. Sister Beatrice was speaking to a policeman. One of the other nuns bent over a young man lying in the middle of the street. Cécile squinted at the still figure. "Someone's fainted," she gasped.

As the girls stepped outside, they heard the policeman's loud voice. "He has the fever, all right," he was saying. "Dropped right in front of the wagon."

Sister Beatrice was shaking her head. "Poor boy. He must be taken to Charity Hospital at once."

Cécile glanced at Marie-Grace with alarm. "I thought the epidemic was over!"

"Papa says it's *almost* over," Marie-Grace assured her. "He says there are fewer cases every day." Marie-Grace's father was a very good doctor; he had helped

Armand get well. Cécile nodded and slowly turned back to the doorway.

Then she heard something—just a small sound, like a whimper. She spun around.

"Did you hear that too?" Marie-Grace asked. "Look." She pointed to an odd trail of items scattered in the street. There was a long *baguette* of French bread, and one, two, three potatoes... The girls followed the path of potatoes, carrots, and onions until they spied a small, hunched figure half-hidden in the shadows at the side of the building.

At first, all Cécile could make out was a pair of thin brown arms clutching a burlap market bag. *That bag must have held the spilled vegetables,* Cécile thought. She could still hear gentle sobbing.

"I'll get Sister Beatrice," Marie-Grace whispered.

Cécile nodded and stepped closer to the shadows. "Hello?" she called softly. "Please come out."

The figure didn't move, but Cécile heard a young girl's voice moan, *"Mon frère..."*

Cécile's heart dropped. *That boy must be her brother!* Cécile looked back at the scene in the street. The young man's limp body had already been lifted onto the back of the wagon. Cécile remembered the day Armand had fallen ill just as suddenly. One moment, he had been painting her portrait in the courtyard—and the next moment, he had collapsed. She had never been so frightened. How scared and alone this little girl must feel!

"*S'il te plaît*—please—come out?" Cécile asked.

The child inched out of the shadows. She looked about seven or eight years old. Her black hair was neatly braided, and her dark eyes were anxious.

"*Comment tu t'appelles?* What is your name?" Cécile asked. She spoke gently, but the girl looked away, watching the wagon roll out of sight.

Cécile waited until it was gone, then tried again. "My name is Cécile," she said. "I know how worried you are. My brother had the fever, too."

This time the girl met her eyes. Cécile reached out her hand, and the child grasped it tightly. "Please tell me your name," Cécile said.

The girl was shaking. She held Cécile's hand tighter. "P-Perrine," she whispered. "Perrine Dupree."

"Where are your parents?" Cécile asked.

Perrine's reply was so soft that Cécile could barely make out the words. "I—I have no one but my brother."

Cécile swallowed hard. *She has already lost her parents...*

Sister Beatrice and Marie-Grace appeared beside them. Cécile quickly explained what she had learned.

Sister Beatrice leaned toward Perrine, her eyes filled with sympathy. "Your brother will be cared for at the hospital," she said. "I will arrange for you to go to Sister Louise. You will be safe with her."

As Sister Beatrice spoke to Perrine, Marie-Grace whispered, "Who's Sister Louise?"

"She's the head of Children of Mercy, the orphanage run by nuns of color. They care for the orphaned girls of color," Cécile murmured. "Maman and I visit there each week, too."

Cécile looked at Perrine again and saw that huge tears were rolling down the little girl's cheeks. Cécile squeezed her hand to reassure her.

"Ah, Perrine," Sister Beatrice said, "you've had quite an upset. Come inside with me and settle down a bit. I will send a message to Sister Louise, and we will get word on how your brother is faring."

"*M-merci*," Perrine stammered. Sister Beatrice turned to lead her away, but Perrine didn't let go of Cécile's hand. "Will you come, too?" she pleaded.

Cécile's heart ached for the little girl, but she hesitated and looked at Marie-Grace. "What about our job?"

"You go ahead," Marie-Grace said. "I think you've got a more important job now."

"Perrine needs a friend," Cécile said softly. "I can do that."

Marie-Grace smiled. "Yes," she agreed. "You know how to be a very good friend."

<hr />

The next morning, Cécile thought of Perrine the minute she woke up. But she would have to wait to find out how the girl was doing. Maman had plans today. She had decided to treat Papa and his crew to a special lunch because they had been working so hard.

The kitchen was busy all morning as Mathilde, the cook, prepared her tastiest dishes. Cécile helped Maman and Tante Octavia pack plates and bowls, glasses and silverware, a tablecloth, and even a vase of bright flowers. Cécile worked eagerly, imagining how happy and pleased Papa, Armand, and the workers would be. Yet she couldn't stop thinking about the little girl with the frightened eyes.

Finally, just before noon, all the baskets had been loaded into the hired carriage. Cécile had just squeezed onto the seat next to her aunt when Maman realized that she'd forgotten the basket of bread.

"I'll get it, Maman." Cécile ran back through the gates that led into the courtyard. There, on the brick path near the lemon tree, was a palmetto basket filled with baguettes. She paused, reminded of Perrine's market bag spilled in the street. *Is Perrine all right? How is her brother?* Cécile wondered for the hundredth time. Then she shook her head and  snatched up the basket. Right now, Papa and his crew were waiting.

"Here it is, Maman." Cécile handed the bread to her mother and scrambled up into the carriage. The driver, Monsieur Antoine, shut the door, and soon the horses were off.

Maman smiled warmly. "Ah, *chérie,* you are such a help to me."

"Oh, I like to be, Maman!" Cécile said, taking the basket back and balancing it on her lap as she spoke.

"Both Sister Beatrice and Sister Louise say that you were a great help with the poor child whose brother fell ill," Tante Tay added.

Cécile sighed, wishing that she had been able to do more. "I didn't talk with her much at all—she was very frightened. But I kept thinking of how I felt when Armand was sick, so I took her hand. And she held on so tight. It was strange—I felt close to Perrine, even though I'd never met her before."

Maman nodded, and the deep blue feather on her hat bobbed toward Cécile's nose. "Sometimes," she said, "just knowing someone cares gives true comfort."

Cécile considered that for a moment. "I would like to visit her. May I, Maman?"

"I am sure that the little girl—"

"Perrine."

"—Perrine would like that. She needs kindness after such a terrible blow."

"And now the orphanages are so crowded," Cécile added, thinking of Perrine alone and frightened among so many strangers.

Maman nodded sadly. "Children of Mercy is bursting at the seams, and so is Holy Trinity and every place that houses the orphaned children."

The carriage turned a corner, and the *clip-clop* of the horses' hooves slowed. Cécile glanced out the window. They were passing a cemetery only a few blocks from Papa's stone yard. The street was clogged with wagons of every size and type, and almost all of them carried long wooden boxes, also of different sizes. As the carriage inched along, Cécile realized that the boxes were coffins . . . coffins for those who had died, like Ellen and Perrine's maman and papa.

Cécile wanted to look away, but she couldn't. For the first time, she understood why Papa had been so very busy lately. He was a stone mason. He carved fancy marble mantels and urns and even fountains . . . and when someone died, if the family could afford it, Papa carved an elegant stone marker and etched the person's name on it.

Monsieur Antoine turned into the winding drive of Papa's stone yard, clucking and coaxing his horses through the tall iron gates. When the carriage came to a stop, Cécile scrambled out first. The gravel of the driveway crunched underneath her boots, and she heard the *clink-clank* of tools ringing out of the wide shop doors.

Cécile watched Maman go into the workshop to kiss Papa on the cheek and greet the workers, but she didn't follow. She didn't want to go inside the workshop, where the tombstones were.

At the side of the drive, Tante Tay spread a tablecloth over two long planks laid across wooden barrels. Monsieur Antoine began to unload the heavy crocks and baskets of food. Cécile caught the scent of spicy turtle soup, but she had lost her appetite. Still clutching the basket of baguettes, she wandered off the gravel drive, into the stone yard.

Papa's stone yard had always been one of her favorite places. Light and shadow bounced off the marble shapes that lived in this garden of stone, each waiting to become something beautiful. She remembered, as a small child, playing hide-and-seek here with Armand. Now Cécile wondered about the children whose parents' names were etched into the stone markers inside Papa's workshop. Would they remember good times with their families, too? Or would they one day forget what it had been like to be in a family?

Cécile leaned against a great block of stone,

shaded from the warm October sun. She listened as the clinking of tools in the workshop stopped and water splashed as the men washed off at the pump. She heard Grand-père's deep, gruff voice, probably telling a joke, and then Armand's laugh, louder than all the others. She heard Maman's soft murmurs, and the tinkle of spoons against bowls. Lunch was being served, but Cécile lingered in the shadows. She couldn't get the orphans out of her mind.

"Cécile!" It was her father's voice. She turned around. Papa had taken off his work smock, but the dust in his dark hair glinted in the sunlight.

"*Oui*, Papa?"

"Maman is looking for the bread, chérie." He reached to take her basket, but then he paused. He raised an eyebrow at her. "Are you all right?"

"I don't know, Papa," she said slowly. She told him about Perrine and about all the other orphans at Holy Trinity and Children of Mercy, whose lives would never be the same after this terrible summer. She tried to put words to the feelings in her heart. "Why . . . why do things have to change?"

Papa squatted down so that he could look into her eyes. Cécile stood very still.

Cécile tried to put words to the feelings in her heart.
"Why . . . why do things have to change?" she asked.

"Everything must change, *ma petite*," Papa said. "Sometimes . . . we don't like it. Sometimes it hurts us, like this yellow fever that changed our family and many others. But change also makes us strong." He paused. "Sometimes it can make us strong enough to do important things."

Cécile could hardly believe it. But if Papa said this, it must be so. "Good things?" she asked.

"Oui. Great things." Papa smiled at her and stood up. It seemed to Cécile that her spirits lifted with him. Papa grasped her soft, small fingers inside his large, rough hand. "Now, come with me to the table. I'm starving!"

Cécile squeezed his hand and began to walk. She felt hopeful suddenly, as if a door had opened inside her mind.

CHAPTER
TWO

AN INVITATION

After supper that evening, there was a knock at the door. "Who can it be at this hour?" Papa wondered.

Cécile jumped up and ran to the hall. She had to use both hands to pull open the heavy cypress door. A boy in a bright red cap stood on the steps in the twilight.

"*Bonsoir.* Good evening," Cécile greeted him.

"Bonsoir." The boy touched his cap in a salute and held out an ivory-colored envelope.

"Maman, a messenger!" Cécile called. Maman's skirts swished as she appeared. Cécile tried her best to see what was written on the envelope as her mother gave the boy a tip and broke the wax seal.

"What is it? Who's it from?" Cécile was so curious that her nose bumped against her mother's sleeve as they walked back to the parlor.

"AWWWK! What is it? Who's it from?" Cécile's pet parrot, Cochon, squawked from his cage.

"*Shhh!*" Maman waved in the bird's direction, and to Cécile's amazement, he clamped his big beak shut.

"It's from Sister Beatrice," Maman said, settling her glasses onto her nose. Everyone—Papa, Grand-père, Armand, Tante Tay, and Tante's little boy, René—had stopped what they were doing to hear what came next.

"The mayor is calling on all citizens to come together on the third Saturday of November for a celebration in Jackson Square. It will be a benefit..."

Maman read silently for a moment and then looked up in wonder.

"...a benefit to raise money for all the children that yellow fever has so cruelly left alone in the world! Sister Beatrice is asking all her friends to help."

"Oh, Maman!" Cécile clapped her hands together.

"With the benefit, we could help *all* the orphans!"

"Yes," Maman agreed. "Let us hope that the benefit will be *very* successful."

"Such a big event will take a lot of work," Papa said. He leaned forward in his chair. "And there's barely a month to do all of it. We must get many people to participate. I'll talk to some of the other businessmen in our community."

"What can *we* do?" Tante Tay asked Maman.

Maman looked at the letter again. "They'll need box lunches to sell, Octavia, dozens and dozens of them. Our club can do some of that." She continued reading. "The ballet company will appear, and the theater troupe will perform. That means there are stages to be built, and stage sets to be painted—"

"Scenery to be painted?" Armand looked up with interest from the corner where he was sketching by gaslight.

"And what can I do?" Cécile asked. Here was her chance to do something truly important to help the children who had lost so much in the epidemic. But no one seemed to hear her question.

"The Philharmonic Society's orchestra will play," Maman went on. "And some of our famous poets and writers will do recitations."

"Oho!" Grand-père sat up straight behind his newspaper. "Here's something about it in the *Daily Picayune*. There will be fireworks at Congo Square. Ah! The soldiers will march!" He suddenly stood at attention. "Certainly I can still fit into my old uniform, *non?*" He patted his stomach and winked.

Armand roared with laughter, but Cécile turned back to her mother.

"Maman, what can *I* do?" she asked again.

Maman gave Cécile a peck on her cheek. "*Ma chérie,* Sister Beatrice says here that the children at the orphanages will make paper flowers and decorations for the stages. You can help them with that."

"Oui, Maman, I will do that, but—" Cécile didn't want to appear ungrateful.

"But what, chérie?" Maman raised a brow.

Papa cast Cécile a knowing look. "Aurélia, I believe ma petite would like to have a greater role in *la célébration.*"

"Hmm." Maman scanned the second page of the letter. "There will be a children's dance troupe... and several children's choirs. Yes, that's it—singing! Cécile, you've progressed so much with Madame

Océane. I'm sure you can sing something quite lovely with one of the choirs!" She smiled proudly.

Cécile blushed. She enjoyed singing, but she was not especially good at it. She was much better at speaking—surely *that* was what she should do. She took a deep breath.

"Maman, I don't want—I mean, I would like to do a recitation instead!"

Cécile's heart began to beat faster as she realized how much she wanted Maman to say yes. Although she had often dreamed of performing onstage, basking in cheers and applause, this was different. Now she didn't really care about getting applause— she simply wanted to help the children.

The children! Cécile caught her breath. *Surely the children will come to the benefit,* she thought. Cécile pictured little Perrine and the children from Holy Trinity sitting in the audience as she spoke. And suddenly she knew *exactly* what she wanted to do for the benefit. She wanted to recite something especially for the children—something that would let them know how much she cared!

Maman's eyes widened. "Public speaking? All by yourself on the stage? Oh, I don't—"

Grand-père cut in. "Surely the child *talks* enough to be good at it, Aurélia!"

Maman looked unconvinced. "After all the money we've spent on singing lessons?"

"Maman!" Armand burst in. He came to his sister's side. "If you allow Cécé to recite a poem, I'll help paint the stage sets."

Cécile grinned at her brother. He was a wonderful artist. Maman peered at the two of them through her eyeglasses.

"You can do this?" Maman asked.

"I want to do it," Cécile said, clasping her hands together nervously. Papa nodded, and she remembered his words in the stone yard. Yes, she was determined to do this good thing!

Maman paused for a moment. "Then you have my blessing." Cécile threw her arms around Maman's neck.

"Cécile," Maman said, "the benefit is important. You must do a very good job. Get help from Monsieur Lejeune to pick your selection, oui?"

"Oui, Maman!" Cécile promised.

The next morning Cécile was in the parlor for her lessons ten minutes early. Monsieur Lejeune arrived at nine o'clock sharp. He seemed delighted with the news of La Célébration.

"Certainly, you should do a recitation," Monsieur Lejeune squeaked in his high voice.

"I want to do a piece that's perfect for the benefit. Maman said I should ask you to suggest something," Cécile said. She tried to look over his shoulder as he rummaged through his battered leather valise.

"Your maman is correct, as always! We must find something just right for a girl of your age, just right for the occasion," he said, turning to shove a stack of unruly papers into Cécile's arms. "Hold these. Aha!" He waved a small book in the air. "Here—*Les Cenelles*."

Cécile stared curiously at the little volume. "What is it?"

Monsieur Lejeune tapped the book. "This, Mademoiselle Cécile, is a collection of poetry written by the finest poets of color in New Orleans."

Cécile was very impressed. "Oh! May I look?" she asked.

Monsieur Lejeune placed the book into Cécile's

hands as if it were a precious jewel. She turned the pages carefully. She saw poems about love, about freedom, about flowers, but nothing seemed just right.

"Here's one I like," she said at last. "It's called 'Response,' by Monsieur Auguste Populus." She began to read the beautiful words in a soft voice, thinking of their meaning.

> *When the thunder has ceased, and the sky,*
> > *now beautiful,*
> *Adorns herself again in her azure dress;*
> *When, smiling of hope, the radiant sun*
> *Throws away its veil and spreads its light upon us,*
> *The happy nightingale joyously sings for us!*

Cécile smiled at the idea of the sky as a lady wearing a blue dress. And the line about the nightingale singing reminded her of Madame Océane's wedding. Surely the children would like a poem that spoke so beautifully about hope and joy returning after a terrible storm.

"*Professeur,* I think I'd like to do this one," she said, continuing to read silently.

"Ah, yes," Monsieur Lejeune said. "The epidemic

was frightening, much like thunder, wasn't it? You've made a good choice, Cécile."

A few hours later, Armand dropped Cécile off at Children of Mercy Orphanage, where nuns took care of free girls of color who'd lost their families. Cécile heard an excited buzz coming from the dining room, just off the entry hall. Girls of every size were working at tables or seated near windows, all busily sewing. A tall nun sat in the center of the group, inspecting someone's work. Cécile watched the girls for a minute, their heads bent over their sewing and their needles flashing in the sunlight. In a crowded classroom across the hall, girls were rolling out huge bolts of cotton on a table and measuring out lengths of fabric with wooden yardsticks.

So many orphans, Cécile thought. But she didn't see Perrine anywhere.

"Bonjour, Cécile!" Sister Louise appeared, wearing an apron over her long black habit. "Have you heard about the benefit? It is a gift from God, non? Our girls are making table linens and pillowcases to sell."

27

Cécile nodded. "I've come to see Perrine, Sister. Is she here?"

The nun's joyful expression became more serious. "She is upstairs, poor child. We have not gotten a word from her since she arrived. Her brother is out of danger, but he won't be able to care for her properly for some time. Go, see if you can cheer her."

Cécile took a deep breath. "I'll do my best," she said, starting up the narrow stairs.

In a small room near the top of the stairs, Perrine sat on a small stool squeezed between an iron bed and the window. She stared down at the street, as if she expected someone.

"Perrine!" Cécile called brightly. "Did you see me coming?" she asked, though she knew that the girl had probably been wishing to see her brother. Perrine turned and nodded slowly.

Cécile perched on the windowsill. What could she say to comfort Perrine? When Armand and Ellen were sick, Cécile remembered, she had wished that they could all be far away from trouble, far from sickness . . . someplace safe and happy. Perhaps Perrine felt just the same now. Cécile suddenly recalled a tale she'd heard from Grand-père long ago.

"Let's go on a trip!" she said with a mischievous smile.

Perrine raised her eyebrows curiously.

"Do you know how we'll travel?" Cécile waved her arm dramatically. "On a magical flying carpet, that's how!"

Perrine's eyes widened. "Can my brother come, too?" she asked in a soft voice. She'd talked!

"Of course. In make-believe, anything can happen, don't you agree?"

Perrine nodded solemnly again.

"My brother's name is Armand," Cécile said. "What is your brother's name?"

"Villaire," Perrine whispered.

Cécile felt as if the story wanted to leap off her tongue. "Now, Perrine, close your eyes. You and Villaire and I are sailing into the sky on our wonderful magic carpet. Hold on!"

Cécile's amazing carpet soared across a great ocean to a land of purple sunsets and cloud castles. With a flutter of her hands, her pretend world came alive with magical dancing birds and a forest of chocolate trees. By the time the story was over, Perrine's eyes were shining.

Cécile hugged the little girl good-bye. "We'll have another adventure soon," she promised.

Ever so briefly, a smile lit Perrine's face.

For the next two weeks, when Cécile wasn't visiting at the orphanages, she faithfully practiced "Response," reading the poem aloud over and over as she memorized the words. At lessons, her tutor helped her with difficult lines, and in the evenings, Maman or Armand sometimes helped her get a verse just right, following along in the book as she recited from memory. During the afternoons, with the book in her hand, she practiced by herself, circling the flower beds in the courtyard and pacing back and forth in her room. "You're wearing a path in the rug, chérie!" Mathilde had exclaimed. But at last, Cécile could recite all the verses from memory. Now she needed to practice before an audience.

But everyone else in the Rey household was very busy getting ready for La Célébration, too. Maman was off to meetings, planning lunch menus and market lists. Tante Octavia was knitting with girls at both orphanages. When Armand wasn't at the stone yard with Papa, he was painting beautiful backdrops for the actors' performances. Grand-père was helping to build the stages.

One afternoon, just before the supper hour, as Cécile recited to the only audience she could find— a tiny marble statue on the mantel—she caught a glimpse of Armand hurrying up the stairs.

"Armand," she called, "will you be my audience?"

"Sorry, Cécé, I'd like to listen, but I promised to help with some painting this evening." He disappeared up the stairs, and a moment later he raced back down and hurried out, his paintbox and brushes under his arm.

Cécile turned back to the statue and started her poem again. But the statue's expression never changed. Cécile sighed. *Can I really do this?* she wondered. *I need someone to tell me if my recitation sounds good.*

Who had the time to listen . . . and knew her well enough to be honest? Suddenly, Cécile knew exactly who.

Marie-Grace!

31

The next day, Cécile went to Holy Trinity to help the children make flowers for the benefit. Just as she was about to set another paper bouquet into a basket near the door, she heard the unmistakable click of paws on the stone floor of the entrance hall. Cécile peeked out from the dining room to see a huge gray dog and its smiling owner. "Marie-Grace!" Cécile called.

"Cécile!" Marie-Grace hurried from the hall. Her dog, Argos, bounded through the dining room, brushing Cécile's skirts as he ran. Cécile's young helpers jumped up from the worktable and followed him into the courtyard, shouting happily. Cécile watched them start a game of fetch, their paper flowers forgotten. She shrugged and set her flowers into the half-filled basket.

"Oh, I've been waiting to see you!" Cécile said as she and Marie-Grace settled onto a dining-room bench to work on the flowers.

Marie-Grace looked closely into Cécile's eyes. "I can see that you have something on your mind. Is it a secret?"

"No—I need your help, that's all." Cécile began to twist wire crookedly around white paper petals.

"What is it?" Marie-Grace asked, taking Cécile's flower and straightening it out before beginning a flower of her own.

"Well, I've decided to recite a poem for La Célébration. You know about the benefit, don't you?"

Marie-Grace looked up brightly. "Yes, of course. Aunt Océane is going to sing—she feels strong enough to perform again! And, Cécile, a poem is such a good idea. You'll be wonderful!"

"Would you listen to me practice?"

Marie-Grace nodded eagerly.

Cécile tried the first few lines. Her mouth was dry. She blushed.

"Try again," Marie-Grace encouraged her.

So Cécile stood and walked around the room, just as she did when she practiced at home. She began again, "When the thunder has ceased..." and this time, the words flowed. Cécile sailed through the first verse and the next, doing her best to put feeling into every word. She stumbled a bit on the last verse, but then she pulled the words from her memory and finished strongly. She could see that she had held Marie-Grace's attention all the way through.

"Brava!" Marie-Grace clapped. "Isn't that what

"I've decided to recite a poem for the benefit," Cécile said.
"Would you listen to me practice?"

the audience calls out after a great performance?"

"Yes!" Cécile laughed with relief. *"Merci beaucoup.* Thank you very much. You are a very good audience." And then, filled with the success of the moment, Cécile grinned impishly. "What are *you* doing for the benefit?" she asked.

"I'm making flowers!" Marie-Grace answered. She twirled a perfect pink bloom.

Cécile gave her a quick look. "If Mademoiselle Océane—I mean, Madame Océane—is singing, why don't you sing with her? You could sing a duet!"

"Me?" Marie-Grace looked surprised.

"Yes, you! You did a beautiful job at the wedding. Everyone thought so."

"I don't know . . ." She looked doubtful.

Cécile smiled. "Marie-Grace, you were born to sing!"

It was Marie-Grace's turn to go pink in the face.

"Ask Madame Océane," Cécile urged. "I'm sure she won't say no. You'll be magnifique together!" Cécile had learned that underneath Marie-Grace's shyness was an adventurous heart, just like her own.

JUST THE
WRONG THING

On Sunday morning, Cécile and
her parents went to Mass at Saint
Louis Cathedral. For the first time
in months, the pews were so full that latecomers had
to squeeze in—one more sign that the long epidemic
was finally ending. The hymns seemed more joyful,
and the candles brighter, now that the church was
full again.

Outside the church after Mass, families stopped
to greet and console one another or catch up on
news. Cécile heard the word "benefit" buzz over and
over as she stood on her toes, looking for girls she
knew. She hadn't seen most of her friends in months,
not since the epidemic began. Soon she spotted the

familiar red ribbon on her good friend Monette Bruiller's favorite bonnet.

"Monette!" Cécile called.

Monette popped out from a cluster of her older brothers. "Cécile! I just heard that you're going to do a recitation at the benefit. To perform in front of a big audience—oh, you are so brave! I would be much too nervous to do such a thing." She slipped her arm through Cécile's and gave her an excited squeeze.

Before Monette could say more, a shadow fell across them. "The trim on that lady's dress is *so* out of fashion!" said a haughty voice. It was Fanny Metoyer, arm in arm with her sister, Agnès. Trailing behind them were a few other girls Cécile knew, listening hungrily.

Cécile turned back to Monette. "Yes, I'm learning a poem to recite at La Célébration!" she said, a bit too loudly. A few people glanced in her direction. She hoped her mother hadn't heard.

Fanny turned back to look at her, surprised. "Why, Cécile! You mean you'll be onstage—with the famous people?" She paused, and her eyes brightened as if she saw Cécile in some new way.

"I certainly hope you've ordered a new dress," Agnès said.

"*I'll* be wearing my new pink frock to the benefit," one of the other girls piped up.

How could these girls be thinking of such unimportant things? Cécile wanted to make a sharp reply, but she bit back the words. Maman always said that a true lady behaved well even at difficult times.

"Oh well," Agnès smirked. "I doubt many people will listen to a stuffy old poem anyway! Come on, Fanny, it's almost time for tea." She swished her skirt and pranced away. The other girls bounced around her like silly puppies, Cécile thought as she stared after them.

"Don't worry about them," Monette said, taking Cécile's hand. They walked for a few minutes without speaking, but Cécile's feelings were tumbling.

Those girls didn't understand anything! Their families had left the city at the first hint of trouble this summer, and they had returned only when the epidemic was over. Now they expected her to giggle over the latest fashions from France and forget that her brother had almost died. They wanted her to sip tea, when she was helping to serve soup to other children who had lost everything. How could they be so uncaring?

A cool breeze stung Cécile's cheeks, and she realized that there were tears on them. She hurriedly wiped them away with the back of her glove.

"Those silly girls don't matter, Cécile," Monette said gently. "Forget about them. Please, tell me about your poem."

Sweet Monette! Cécile sniffed through her tears and tried to smile. Then she thought again of what Fanny and Agnès had said. They didn't really have any idea what the terrible summer had been like. They couldn't imagine how frightening the worst hours and days had been. If they heard her recite the poem, would they even understand why she had chosen it? Or would they simply think she was onstage to show off?

That night, Cécile lay awake worrying. How many people in the audience would be like Fanny and Agnès? How many people would completely misunderstand her reason for performing? Even if she said her poem perfectly, would she touch their hearts at all?

Finally, unable to sleep, Cécile went out to the balcony, where the breeze was cooler. She stared out at the moonlit courtyard.

Suddenly she remembered standing with Marie-Grace just a few weeks before, looking out on the courtyard of Holy Trinity Orphanage. She pictured the children waiting for their morning treat. She remembered how, only a few minutes later, she and Marie-Grace had rushed downstairs, and she had met Perrine...

All at once, Cécile's mind felt clear. It was for Perrine and the other orphans that she was reciting. As long as her poem made them happy, nothing else really mattered, did it?

Cécile took a deep breath. There was just one more person she would ask to listen to her poem. If that went well, she would be ready for the benefit.

She had to see Perrine as soon as she could!

Right after lessons the next day, Cécile went with Maman to Children of Mercy. While Maman delivered a bolt of linen fabric to Sister Louise, Cécile slipped away to look for Perrine.

As usual, the little girl was alone upstairs, sitting beside the window. She turned when she heard Cécile's footsteps. Though her eyes seemed to light up, she didn't speak.

"Perrine! I want to share something with you." Cécile hurried to her side.

"A story?" Perrine asked in a small voice, smiling hopefully.

"No . . . not quite. It's a poem. Would you like to hear it?"

Perrine gazed up, her eyes bright with anticipation. Cécile stood straight, cleared her throat, and began. She had never recited more smoothly, or with more feeling. She was completely caught up in the poem. Finally, clasping her hands together near her heart, she delivered the last lines:

> *Celebrate with your songs this great victory;*
> *Your return to virtue crowns you with glory!*

As she finished, Cécile felt certain that even Monsieur Populus himself would have been proud of her. She smiled expectantly at her special audience. "Well, Perrine, what do you think?" she asked.

But Perrine was looking out the window, not at Cécile. "I . . . I didn't understand it," she murmured.

Cécile was stunned. She'd thought everything was perfect. The words of the poem were beautiful. Her voice had been steady and even and full of feeling. And yet, the poem had meant nothing to the audience that mattered most.

Perrine pulled at her sleeve. "Tell me one of your stories instead?"

Suddenly, Cécile had no voice at all, except the one inside her head telling her what she already knew: If Perrine didn't understand, neither would the other children. "I can't," Cécile gasped. "I must go."

Cécile rushed away with her insides shaking. She couldn't tell which she felt more terrible about: disappointing Perrine, or knowing that the great thing she had planned for La Célébration had turned out to be all wrong.

Later that week, Cécile and Marie-Grace folded laundry in the music-room-turned-dormitory at Holy Trinity. Rain began to patter against the windows. The sudden shower was strong and steady, bringing nuns and children hurrying inside. Cécile listened to the sounds of children settling into the dining room downstairs to complete the garden of paper flowers.

"What if it rains next week? What if people don't come to the benefit?" Cécile said as she looked outside anxiously. She didn't have the courage to tell her friend what she was *really* worried about.

"I'm sure the weather will be fine," Marie-Grace reassured her. "Are you ready for the big day?"

Cécile swallowed and then shook her head. "Perrine didn't like the poem!" she blurted out.

Marie-Grace's eyes widened in surprise. "But it's such a beautiful poem, and you recite it so well. Whatever happened?"

Cécile hesitated. "As nice as the poem is, I don't think the children will understand it." She sighed. "I chose the poem just for them. I thought it would make them feel happy and . . . and hopeful. But I'm afraid they won't understand it at all." She took a deep breath, and her throat felt tight. "Now I don't know what to do."

Marie-Grace looked thoughtful. "Cécile, I have an idea. When you make up stories, all the children love to listen to you. So . . . what if you say your own words at the benefit?"

Cécile stared at her. "You mean that I should tell a story?"

"Well, no, maybe not a story. But you could write your own poem. You could write it especially for the children."

Cécile frowned. "Writing is so hard. I'm not very good at it."

"But you wrote letters to Armand every week for nearly two years," Marie-Grace pointed out. "And writing a poem is better than writing a letter, where you only tell about things that happened. A poem can be about your feelings, can't it?"

"But—but I've never written a poem before!" Cécile said. "And the benefit is less than a week away! I don't know . . ."

Marie-Grace smiled encouragingly. "When you told me I should sing a duet with Aunt Océane, I was nervous at first, too. But the benefit is important, so

I decided to try. Now I've discovered how much I enjoy singing with Aunt Océane, and that makes it easier." She touched Cécile's arm. "Your idea was right for me. Maybe my idea will be right for you."

Cécile glanced away and tried to swallow the lump of worry in her throat.

A few minutes later, Armand came to collect Cécile. Her spirits felt as gray as the clouds, but when she'd said her good-byes and stepped outside, her brother didn't seem to notice. With a grin, he gave his huge black parasol a twirl and then pulled a note from his waistcoat and passed it to her.

"For me?" Cécile asked, looking closely at the unfamiliar, spidery writing of her name.

"Ah, oui! Get used to receiving admiring notes," he laughed. "After your performance, you're sure to receive many."

Cécile didn't look at him as she tore open the envelope and read the brief message inside.

"It's from Sister Louise!" Her heart thumped. "She writes that she and Perrine will be in the front row for my performance." Cécile crumpled the paper, imagining Perrine's little face staring up at her in confusion. Not so long ago, she'd wanted nothing more than for Perrine to be in the audience. But now . . .

Armand didn't seem to notice Cécile's reaction. "I hear that the children from Holy Trinity will also attend," he said. "And of course your whole family will be there, too. Your most adoring audience must see the star's performance up close!" He smiled good-naturedly.

Cécile tried to smile back, but her stomach quivered. What was she going to do? If she recited "Response," the children wouldn't understand. But if she wrote her own poem, would it be good enough? Would Maman be disappointed? Maman's words echoed in her head: *The benefit is important. You must do a very good job.*

Tears blurred her eyes. Why, oh why, had she ever thought she could do this?

GIFTS AND DREAMS

"How is it going, chérie?" Maman called to Cécile from the hallway the next morning. Maman smiled and arranged her hat as she looked in the hall mirror.

"Fine, Maman," Cécile answered untruthfully. She was heading toward the courtyard with *Les Cenelles* in her hand. She had spent hours looking through the little book, searching without success for a poem that would be easier for Perrine and the other children to understand. Marie-Grace's suggestion kept coming back to her, but Cécile couldn't seriously consider it—not with only three days left!

Maman slipped what looked like a long list into her purse. "I am going. Madame Bruiller and I must arrange a fair price for the meat that our club will be serving at the food tent." Maman blew Cécile a kiss. "Keep practicing, chérie. We're all working very hard, but we remember that it's for the best of causes, non?" She gave a final wave and left.

The best of causes. Cécile swallowed hard. How could she give *her* best for the benefit? It seemed impossible now.

She wandered across the courtyard. She had no choice left but to recite the poem she had chosen with her tutor, she decided sadly. She must do the best she could with it. Perhaps she could practice for Mathilde.

The cook stood at the wide wooden worktable in the kitchen, holding a scoop of shelled pecans in one hand. The table was spread with bowls.

Mathilde's kind brown eyes smiled at her. "Reciting again?" she asked, glancing at the little book in Cécile's hand. Cécile nodded miserably.

Mathilde squinted at her. "Perhaps you are working at it too hard, chérie. Come, take a break. Help me get the spices ready for my cakes."

Cécile was happy to linger in the warm room with Mathilde. Maman always said that Mathilde was the best cook in the city, but her cakes came straight from heaven. Today, Mathilde was making twenty—twenty!—fruitcakes to sell at the benefit.

Mathilde wiped a floury hand on her apron and patted Cécile's shoulder. "If you are a good helper, maybe I will give you a little sample of my cake."

Cécile pressed against the table's edge. There were shelled pecans and dark raisins to chop and cinnamon sticks to be crushed. Knobby fingers of gingerroot and brown nutmegs were waiting to be grated. She closed her eyes for a second, almost tasting the flavors blended into a sweet, moist slice of cake.

Cécile opened her eyes and picked up one of the small, round nutmegs. As she began to grate it, the delicious smell of the spice surrounded them.

"Mathilde," Cécile asked, "how did you become so good at cooking?"

"Don't know. My *grand-mère* took me into the kitchen when I was small, let me taste and smell. Very soon I was standing on a stool, cooking!"

"Just like that, you did it?" Cécile couldn't resist stopping to swipe a few raisins to pop into her mouth.

Mathilde folded her arms and gave Cécile a warning look. Then she smiled so that her eyes crinkled at the corners. "Grand-mère said I had a gift for cooking."

"A gift?" Cécile felt puzzled. "But a gift is—"

"—not always what you think. It can be something that comes natural to a person." Mathilde stopped, glancing at Cécile's confused frown. "I see food, I smell seasonings, and I just know what goes together and tastes good." She chuckled softly. "That doesn't mean I always got things right at first, but I liked to practice and learn. Cooking is easy for me. My grand-mère was right—it's my gift. It makes me happy, and it lets me make other people happy, too."

Cécile slowly pushed the nutmeg back and forth against the grater. What was it Marie-Grace had said about singing with Madame Océane? She enjoyed it because it was easy . . . or it was easy because she enjoyed it?

"I want to make people happy," Cécile said. "That's why I want to get my poem right. I want to do my very best!" She grated faster and faster as she spoke.

"Watch, now!" Mathilde put a gentle hand on Cécile's arm to stop her from grating so furiously. Cécile looked at her sheepishly.

"I see food, I smell seasonings, and I just know what goes together,"
Mathilde explained. "Cooking is easy for me. It's my gift."

"Everything is best when you put love inside, chérie."

"Everything?" Cécile asked, setting the grater down. Mathilde lifted the small bowl and dumped the powdery spice into her batter.

"Yes, indeed," she said, turning to Cécile and looking unexpectedly serious. "Everything!"

That night, Cécile dreamed that she was standing on the clouds, and all around her was bright blue sky. A flock of birds surprised her. The sweet, singing nightingales fluttered their wings all at once, and Cécile laughed with joy.

Then, in the blink of an eye, the birds changed into people! Mathilde and Marie-Grace and Monette were there, and Maman and Tante Tay and even Perrine. They were smiling and hugging her; she felt their love and she loved them back. Something soft brushed her cheek. It was a feather from Maman's hat. Maman plucked the feather out of her hat and held it out to Cécile.

"Your gift," Maman whispered to her.

Cécile looked up to thank her mother, but she was gone. When Cécile looked down again, the feather had changed. It had become a writing pen.

Cécile's eyes flew open.

Her gift! Suddenly she understood. She loved to talk and tell stories, just as Grand-père had said. Words were her gift—the words that came from her own heart and mind. It was easy for her to make people happy with her words.

All at once, Marie-Grace's advice made sense, and Cécile knew what she must do. She threw back her covers, drew a shawl over her shoulders, and headed for her brother's room. His door at the end of the balcony was closed. Cécile rapped impatiently.

"Who's there?" Armand called sleepily.

"It's me, Cécile!" she whispered, rubbing her hands together against the brisk early-morning air.

Armand swung the door open. He was wearing his nightshirt and robe. "Cécé! Is something wrong?"

"Non! *Écoute*—listen! I need to borrow something to write with."

"What?" Armand stifled a yawn. "Whatever are

you writing in the middle of the night?"

"It's almost morning. And I'm going to write my own poem for La Célébration!"

Armand snapped wide-awake. "You only have a few days! Does Maman know?"

She shook her head. "No one except you. Please, may I have—"

"Of course. *Une minute.*" He turned away but came back quickly, shoving a roll of paper and a drawing pencil into Cécile's hands. "Are you sure about this?" he asked.

"Oh, yes!" she said. "Merci. Merci beaucoup!"

Cécile tiptoed down the back stairs to the courtyard. The morning light was rising with a soft glow over the rooftops. She looked up at the pale sky, and then she sat at the little iron table and began to write. The words flowed. Some she crossed out, but she tried others until they were just right.

She knew that she wouldn't need to memorize this poem, because each word was imprinted on her heart.

La Célébration

"Papa, this is like Mardi Gras season!" Cécile squeezed her father's hand as they stepped from a narrow side street into Jackson Square. It was pulsing with people. Flags snapped in the breeze, and garlands of paper flowers draped a large stage just ahead. Nearby, an orchestra played lively music.

Cécile scanned the square, her eyes wide at the enormous crowd that had turned out for the benefit. Her heart swelled as she realized that all these people were here to help the orphaned children of New Orleans. Her performance was in less than an hour. She was excited and eager—and nervous, too.

"Tilde's cakes! Tilde's cakes!" a marchande called

nearby, her bright kerchief fluttering.

"Do you think she means Mathilde's cakes?" asked Armand, arching his neck as René, who was perched on his shoulders, held on for his life.

"Surely they can be no one else's," Tante Tay laughed.

"Hold on tight, René. We're cake hunters!" Armand said, plunging into the crowd. Cécile wanted to push into the crowd behind them, but she looked down at her new dress. She'd better keep it nice for her performance. She had decided to surprise Maman with the new poem, and that was going to be enough of a shock. Cécile thought she'd better not surprise Maman with a dirty dress, too!

Strolling slowly with Papa and Tante Tay, Cécile took in the great spectacle in Jackson Square. Everywhere people chatted and laughed, munched delicious-smelling treats, and crowded toward rows of benches lined up before stages. A cluster of excited girls wearing dancing skirts and slippers hurried past, ready to perform. The soaring notes of an opera rose up from a large wooden stage. Cécile passed another stage where actors in long Roman robes were performing a dramatic scene. Behind them, a huge painted backdrop showed a marble temple gleaming in an imaginary sun. The temple looked so real that Cécile felt as if she could walk right inside. She caught her breath—was that Armand's painting?

Tante Tay touched Cécile's shoulder and pointed her gloved hand in the direction of the cathedral. "See the white tents?" she asked. "That's where your maman is selling the box lunches. All the food tents are busy. There's one selling French pastries and one selling fried shrimp. The Ladies' Opera Society is brave, I've heard—they're trying to sell candies. I don't believe they can outdo Madame Zulime's pralines!"

So many people have given their gifts to the benefit, Cécile thought. Bakers and carpenters, actors, artists, dancers, musicians. La Célébration had brought together people from every neighborhood in the city. Cécile heard French and Spanish, English and German. Faces of every color mingled together in the crowd.

She couldn't stop looking. It seemed that for this special day, everyone had forgotten their differences. All of New Orleans had turned out to help the orphans!

And soon, Cécile realized, it would be her turn

to share *her* gift. A shiver ran through her.

"What time is it, Papa? I don't go on until two-thirty, but Madame Océane and Marie-Grace sing at two, and I don't want to miss them!"

Papa stopped to check his pocket watch. "It's almost two o'clock, ma petite." He scanned the square. "Grand-père is to meet us right here in just a few minutes," he said. "Which stage—"

"They sing on Stage Four, the same one that I'm on. Hurry!" Cécile tugged at her father's arm.

"Won't you wait for an old man?" Grand-père's booming voice was clear, even with the other noises around them. Cécile looked over her shoulder. Grand-père swept his tall navy hat off his silver head and stuck out his chestful of brass buttons.

She slowed for him, laughing. "You're the most handsome grand-père in New Orleans!" she said.

He cocked one ear. "Say that again? I didn't quite hear," he joked.

As Cécile led the way, little butterflies began fluttering in her stomach. She was relieved to see that Stage Four was much smaller than the one where the orchestra played. It was decorated with ribbon streamers and festooned with boughs of cypress.

Tucked into the feathery branches were yellow and pink paper flowers. At one end of the stage, three musicians warmed up. A good-sized crowd was getting seated on the benches in front of the stage. The crowd's lively chatter made a buzz in the air.

Her heart thumping with excitement, Cécile made her way right up to the very front of the small wooden stage. She leaned around Grand-père and glanced back at the audience. Perrine and the other orphans were nowhere in sight. Would they arrive in time for her performance? They *had* to—the poem was for them! Cécile blew out a breath. Nearby she caught sight of Marie-Grace's uncle, Monsieur Luc Rousseau, and her father, Dr. Gardner, already seated in the front row. They were talking together and didn't look up until a man wearing a fancy swallowtail coat stepped to the center of the stage.

"Mesdames et messieurs. Ladies and gentlemen," he said. The crowd began to quiet down. "I now introduce to you one of New Orleans' most promising young sopranos, Madame Océane Michel Rousseau! Accompanying her in a duet is a newcomer to the stage, Mademoiselle Marie-Grace Gardner!"

He backed off the stage, and two violinists

began to play. Out walked Madame Océane and Marie-Grace, wearing just-alike dresses in a blue that matched Madame Océane's eyes.

"How lovely they look together," Maman whispered as she slipped into place next to Cécile.

A hush fell over the crowd as Madame Océane began to sing in pure, sweet notes. Marie-Grace joined in softly. Cécile held her breath. They were perfect together.

When the last notes of the duet disappeared, the audience applauded furiously. Madame Océane bowed graciously. Marie-Grace caught Cécile's eye and beamed. Someone shouted for an encore, and Cécile thought she recognized that voice as Monsieur Luc's.

"You were magnifique!" Cécile whispered when her friend came offstage.

"Thank you," Marie-Grace said, flushed with excitement and happiness. Then she took Cécile's hand and smiled. "You'll be wonderful too, Cécile. I'm sure of it!"

"I took your advice," Cécile whispered with a nervous smile. Marie-Grace's brows arched with surprise as her uncle gently pulled her away to give her a warm hug.

"Cécile!" a small voice called from close by.

Cécile looked around and finally saw a small, dark-eyed girl clinging to Sister Louise's skirts.

"Cécile!" Perrine squealed her name again and ran to wrap her arms around Cécile's neck.

"I'm so glad to see you," Cécile whispered.

Perrine stepped back and tugged Cécile's sleeve. "I brought my brother," she said.

Cécile looked up again. Standing nearby was a thin young man with curly brown hair. He placed one hand on Perrine's shoulder and dipped his head in a greeting.

The swallowtailed man started speaking again. "Our next performer will recite a poem. I present to you—Mademoiselle Cécile Amélie Rey!"

Cécile took a deep breath.

Bonne chance!" Marie-Grace wished her good luck in perfect French and gave her a nudge.

Cécile walked up the steps and crossed the stage. She stopped in the center and turned to the crowd. It was like standing alone on a tiny island in the middle of the Mississippi River. For a moment, the sea of faces all looking up at her made her feel dizzy.

Cécile breathed deeply and focused on the first

row of the audience. A cluster of tidy girls and boys, guided by Sister Beatrice, was squeezing in next to Sister Louise and Perrine. Next to them stood Dr. Gardner and Marie-Grace, and Monsieur Luc with Madame Océane on his arm. Maman and Papa were beaming up at her. Armand waved. Grand-père and Tante Tay were pointing her out to René. Mathilde rushed up beside them, still in her cooking apron.

Cécile cleared her throat. "My poem is called 'Things to Hold Close,'" she said, trying to speak clearly.

She took another deep breath and, swallowing back her fears, she began to speak the words she had written from her heart:

> *When summer came and the sun beat down,*
> *A season of sorrow began in our town.*
> *Many people left because they were afraid,*
> *And life in New Orleans changed for all who stayed.*
>
> *Friends and strangers worked together,*
> *Making each other strong,*
> *And the best medicine was a soft voice*
> *Or a gentle song.*

When I see children all alone,
I know the cost.
I feel my heart break
Over what they have lost.

Though I am just a girl to most,
This summer has taught me what to hold close:
Happy memories of the past, our smiles today,
Friends and family beside us, and those far away.

Today we gather to help the children in need.
Under these cloudless skies, our city is great indeed.
My words may be weak, but my feelings are true.
These words—and my love—are my gift to you.

Cécile spread her arms wide at the end. She bowed to the cheering audience.

As she stepped off the stage, a cluster of children from Holy Trinity surrounded her, pressing paper flowers and good wishes on her from every direction.

Then Perrine stood beside her. Her eyes were filled with tears. Cécile's breath caught. Had the poem upset her? But no, Perrine's face was glowing.

"Oh, Cécile, *c'était beau*," she said. "Merci!"

Cécile's heart swelled. Perrine thought her poem

"These words—and my love—are my gift to you," Cécile said.

was beautiful. She had understood the feelings Cécile was trying to express! Cécile suddenly felt tears of happiness spring to her own eyes.

Perrine took her hand and stood on tiptoe so that she could reach Cécile's ear. *"Je t'aime,* Cécile," she whispered shyly.

Cécile put her arm around Perrine. "I love you, too," she answered gently.

All at once, Maman was there. She cupped Cécile's face in both her hands. Cécile began to tremble inside. What was the look on her mother's face? She'd never seen it before. Was Maman unhappy with her?

"Maman, I—"

"Cécile, I—" Maman was so overcome that she couldn't get the words out in English. *"C'était une joie de te voir! Ma fille précieuse!"*

You were a joy to see! My precious daughter! Cécile had never before received such praise from her mother. Her heart almost burst with joy.

CHAPTER
SIX
—

SO LONG FOR NOW

A few evenings later, the Reys
and their guests took their places
in the candlelit dining room. This
special dinner was Cécile's idea. Right after the
benefit, she had asked Papa if Marie-Grace and her
family could come to dinner before they left for
Belle Chênière. Cécile had even promised to help
with the dinner.

Papa had paused for a moment, but then he
had smiled at her. "You have a generous heart, ma
petite," he'd said. "Yes, I will send an invitation to
Dr. Gardner." Cécile knew that Papa was thinking of
Armand and how the fever had almost taken him.
Dr. Gardner had done a lot for their family.

Now, here they all were together. Papa sat at one end of the long table, Grand-père at the other. Armand, Cécile, and Marie-Grace sat on one side with Tante Octavia. Across from them were Maman, Dr. Gardner, Monsieur Luc, and Madame Océane.

Mathilde stood beside the mahogany buffet in her starched white apron, ready to serve. She nodded proudly at Cécile. Cécile smiled back and then bowed her head as Grand-père began the blessing.

"We give thanks for this wonderful meal," he began, his voice bouncing off the papered walls, "and for Mathilde's incredible skills in the kitchen . . . and for our Cécile's many new talents!"

Armand glanced up and winked at Cécile.

"I can't believe you helped cook all this!" Marie-Grace whispered, shaking her head at the variety of dishes.

"I cooked the okra and tomatoes all by myself!" Cécile whispered back. Then she looked down at the brightly colored flowers and birds on her plate.

"We are thankful," Grand-père continued, "that we can be together, family and friends, in this season of recovery." He paused again. This time, Cécile was still. He was talking about Armand and Océane. She heard someone sniff. Was it Mathilde, or Maman?

"And we are thankful for the success of La Célébration. New Orleans truly cares for her children. Merci, *Seigneur*. Thank you, Lord. Amen."

Grand-père's blessing of the meal was over. Mathilde began to pass bowls of tomato bisque.

"Now, is it true, *monsieur le docteur*," Grand-père asked, looking down the table, "that you know just how much money La Célébration has raised?"

"Well," Dr. Gardner said, putting down his spoon, "the money is still being counted. But it seems that New Orleans does care about her children. Every orphanage in the city will be helped!"

Everyone at the table burst into applause. *Now,* thought Cécile with satisfaction, *the children will have plenty to eat—and enough beds and blankets, too.* She caught Marie-Grace's eye, and they shared a smile.

Then everyone turned to the dinner. *Mathilde has done her best ever,* Cécile thought. The buffet was spread with roast duck and wild rice, shrimp and the tomato bisque, okra, dandelion greens, and warm rolls. For a while, there was only eating. Then there was chatting between bites.

Monsieur Luc and Grand-père talked about ships

and riverboats while Océane and Tante Tay discussed music. Just as Cécile swallowed the last of her peach compote, Marie-Grace dropped her voice and said, "You'll see me off at the levee tomorrow, won't you?"

Cécile smiled. "Of course!"

At the same moment, Dr. Gardner cleared his throat to speak. "Monsieur Rey, Madame Rey... thank you for your gracious hospitality. My daughter has found a good friend in your Cécile." He looked lovingly at Marie-Grace. "And I want you to know that I'm very impressed with the efforts of the people here in this city. It makes me both proud and happy to have returned to New Orleans."

Maman beamed and rose from her seat. "Mathilde, we will have *café au lait* in the parlor, please." She led the guests to the front room. Tante Tay went to her harp and began to play softly.

Cécile pulled Marie-Grace upstairs to her room. They laughed and chatted, talking about the dinner and the benefit. Then, carefully, she showed Marie-Grace her most prized possession—Amie, the beautiful porcelain doll that Armand had made for her while he was studying in France.

Marie-Grace looked back and forth between

Cécile's face and Amie's. "Why, you and Amie look exactly alike!" she exclaimed.

Cécile nodded, suddenly remembering how much she had missed Armand during his two years away, and how happy she had been when he'd returned. "Even though we were so far apart," she said slowly, "Armand and I stayed close. We never forgot each other, not even a little."

Marie-Grace linked her arm through Cécile's. "We'll stay close, too. And don't worry—my trip will be *much* shorter than Armand's."

Cécile laughed. She was already looking forward to Marie-Grace's return.

Then Madame Océane called, and the girls went down to the parlor and sang together as their aunts accompanied them. Their voices blended together perfectly with the soft, clear notes of the harp.

In the morning, Cécile was pulling on her hat in the front hall when her grandfather appeared.

"Are you ready?" Grand-père asked, rubbing his hands together. "This weather reminds me of my days at sea. Gets your blood moving!"

He threw open the door, and the cold November air rushed up Cécile's nose, making her laugh. They walked briskly to the river.

It was a busy morning on the levee. Grand-père led her to where the riverboats were docked.

Cécile shaded her eyes against the reflections of light off the water and searched for Monsieur Luc's boat, the *Éléonore*. She had promised herself that she wouldn't cry today, because this wasn't really a good-bye. *À bientôt*, she would say—so long for now.

A riverboat whistle blew, and Cécile jumped.

"Céciiiile!" From far away, she heard her name. She weaved among well-wishers and sailors, hopping up and down to see where the voice was coming from.

"Marie-Grace!" she called.

"Cécile!"

An elegant double-decker riverboat was beginning to inch backward from the dock. On the upper deck, Monsieur Luc and Madame Océane stood together. Madame Océane waved a bouquet of flowers. One deck below, Marie-Grace rushed along the rails.

"À bientôt!" Cécile called. "Enjoy your cousins!"

"What?" Marie-Grace shouted.

Cécile cupped her hands around her mouth. "Have fun!" she called.

Marie-Grace waved madly. Cécile waved back and kept waving until the boat had steamed far enough upriver to sound its horn again.

Cécile's fingers were freezing. She had forgotten her gloves, but she didn't care. She pushed her hands into the pockets of her coat. Having a true friend was a great thing.

A great thing indeed!

Belle Chênière, Louisiana
December 4, 1853

Dear Cécile,

Happy Christmas! I hope you and your family are well. Have you been to Holy Trinity often? How is little Perrine? Is she with her brother again? I miss New Orleans and you, but I am going to have the best Christmas ever. Papa is coming here for the holidays!

Uncle Luc and Aunt Océane and I are staying with my Great-Aunt Lisette, in a house surrounded by trees, just up the hill from the river. I've met so many aunts, uncles, and cousins. My cousins speak French, so my French is getting better, too.

Everyone loves music here, so we sing together in the evenings—and Aunt Océane plays for us. (I love writing "Aunt Océane"!) I've learned some songs that my mother used to sing. I hope you and I can sing them together when we have voice lessons again.

I wanted to tell you something. When I heard the poem you wrote, I knew that you were a real writer. I think someday you'll be famous!

Please write soon and tell me everything that is happening in New Orleans. I'm so looking forward to seeing you when I return home. I hope we'll have more adventures together!

Your sincere friend,
Marie-Grace Gardner

82 Dumaine Street
New Orleans, Louisiana
December 12, 1853

Dear Marie-Grace,

You see, I kept my promise. I am writing back to you! Thank you for saying nice things about my poem. I am trying to write another poem, but I'm not sure it's very good. Maman says it is, but she's my mother!

I told René you were busy riding alligators on the bayou. I think he believed me! He was very impressed. I could write a story about that, non?

I go to Holy Trinity once a week. The children always ask for Marie-the-Great. I told them you and I would chase them around the courtyard again very soon. Perrine's brother has recovered from the fever, and Papa has given him a job at the stone yard. I am helping Perrine learn to read!

And don't worry—I'll save some adventures just for you, because you're such a good friend. Maman says true friends are friends forever. We are, aren't we?

Your friend,
Cécile Amélie Rey

People donating money to help victims of a yellow fever epidemic that swept through the South in 1878

Many communities in Cécile's time faced disasters such as epidemics, fires, floods, hurricanes, and tornadoes, just as towns and cities do today. But 150 years ago, there were no government programs or national organizations like the Red Cross to help when disaster struck. Instead, people depended mostly on their own neighbors and community for help.

Often, religious congregations or local businesspeople led efforts to help by collecting money for food, medical services, or building supplies. Friends and strangers pitched in to help, too, just as Cécile and her family do in the story.

A volunteer receives supplies to help victims of an epidemic in Memphis, Tennessee.

The terrible yellow fever epidemic that swept through New Orleans in 1853 was one of the worst disasters that any American city had ever faced. Nearly 10,000 people died in only a few months—so many that almost everyone in the city lost family members or friends. Yet those who survived reached out with amazing courage and generosity to nurse the sick and help people in need.

A nun arriving to help a family struck by yellow fever. Some brave volunteers fell ill with the fever themselves.

As the epidemic drew to an end, New Orleans faced a fresh crisis—caring for the thousands of orphaned children whose parents had died of yellow fever.

A number of orphanages in the city were run by women dedicated to providing good care for the children. For example, Henriette Delille *(duh-leel)* was a well-to-do woman of color who founded the Sisters of the Holy Family, a Catholic order of African American nuns that still serves the poor today. Much like the fictional Sister Louise in the story, she established an orphanage for girls of color. An Irish immigrant named Margaret Haughery *(HAW-ry)* was another woman who dedicated her life to

Henriette Delille, who founded an orphanage for girls of color

helping New Orleans' poor. Orphaned as a child herself, she lost her only daughter to yellow fever. She estab-

After Margaret Haughery died, a statue of her was erected in front of this New Orleans orphanage.

lished four orphanages, including one that opened after the yellow fever epidemic of 1853.

Yet even remarkable women like these needed help to keep their orphanages running after the epidemic. By the fall of 1853, every orphanage in New Orleans was bursting at the seams and desperately needed food, clothing, fuel, and other supplies to care for the huge number of newly orphaned children.

The people of New Orleans responded to this new crisis with great generosity, even though many had closed their businesses and lost their incomes during the epidemic. As soon as newspapers ran articles about the orphanages' needs, donations poured in— first from New Orleans and then, as the news spread, from Americans all across the country.

To raise more money for the orphanages, volunteers organized benefits much like the one in Cécile's story. The benefits usually took place in the city's beautiful parks and gardens and featured both professional and amateur performers, including singers,

In Cécile's time, benefits often featured performances of classical music, drama, and poetry. This illustration shows a fund-raising concert held in 1853.

dancers, musicians, and actors. Poetry recitations were also very popular. One fund-raiser, called "Remember the Orphans," promised the biggest fireworks display the city had ever seen. At another benefit, orphans themselves sang, waltzed, and recited poems. For every event, large crowds turned out to enjoy the performances and help the children. The benefits not only raised much-needed money, they also helped bring life and joy back to the city.

Child actors, costumed for the stage

Americans across the country admired the spirit with which New Orleans recovered from the epidemic. Even in faraway cities such as Baltimore and Philadelphia, newspapers praised the city's courage and determination.

*Saint Charles Theater, one of New Orleans' many theaters and opera houses. The arts—
music, dance, theater, and literature—were extremely popular in the city.*

It is not surprising that the people of New Orleans turned to the arts to help their city recover. By the time Cécile was born, New Orleans had become one of the leading cultural centers of the United States. Girls like Cécile and Marie-Grace regularly went to the city's luxurious theaters to attend operas, ballets, concerts, and plays in both English and French. In Cécile's time, New Orleans produced some of America's most distinguished composers and musicians.

In a city filled with people of different backgrounds and ethnic heritages, a great variety of artistic traditions flourished. African and

*New Orleans theatergoers enjoyed
shows by renowned performers such
as the great singer Jenny Lind.*

These professional musicians from Cécile's time played banjo, guitar, and violin. They probably performed dance music in theaters and homes.

Caribbean music pulsed from city squares. Black spirituals and the work chants of enslaved people sounded on the docks. At dances and balls, both black and white orchestras played popular European dance music such as polkas and waltzes. By the late 1800s, brass bands filled the streets with lively music for parades, steamboat arrivals, and funerals.

Inspired by the rich mix of traditions around them, New Orleans musicians began borrowing and blending elements from all of them to create new styles of music. By the early twentieth century, New Orleans had given rise to jazz. Now enjoyed around the globe, jazz is considered one of America's greatest musical contributions to the world.

In a similar way, New Orleans developed a famous cooking style that grew out of the city's mix of cultures. Its deliciously seasoned dishes use fresh seafood, rice, vegetables, and herbs from Louisiana, prepared in ways that reflect French, Spanish, African, Caribbean, Native American, and other influences. The result

In the 20th century, New Orleans native Louis Armstrong was one of the world's most famous and influential jazz musicians.

is a unique style of cooking that is admired around the country.

In the years since Cécile's story, New Orleans has faced other disasters, such as Hurricane Katrina in 2005 and a major oil spill in the nearby

Jambalaya, one of New Orleans' best-known dishes, features shrimp, sausage, chicken, rice, vegetables, and delicious seasonings.

Gulf of Mexico in 2010. Yet the city's special character, strong community spirit, and rich heritage still thrive.

If you visit New Orleans today, you can hear the sounds of jazz musicians and brass bands in the streets. You can see French- and Spanish-style architecture in the older areas of the city, watch great ships on the Mississippi River, and walk the aisles of the French Market to shop for fresh produce and baked goods, just as Cécile and Marie-Grace did. And you can enjoy wonderful restaurants that serve gumbo, jambalaya, and the other traditional dishes that Mathilde might have prepared for Cécile's family.

New Orleans' unique heritage still lives on today.

Glossary of French Words

à bientôt *(ah byehn-toh)*—good-bye for now, see you again soon

baguette *(bah-get)*—a long, thin loaf of French bread

bonjour *(bohn-zhoor)*—hello

bonne chance *(bun shahnss)*—good luck

bonsoir *(bohn-swar)*—good evening

café au laît *(kah-fay oh lay)*—coffee with milk

C'ést impossible. *(set ahm-poh-see-bluh)*—It's impossible.

C'était beau. *(say-teh boh)*—It was beautiful.

C'était une joie de te voir! *(say-teh ewn zhwah duh tuh vwar)*—
It was a joy to see you.

chérie *(shay-ree)*—dear, darling. *Ma chérie* means "my dear."

Comment tu t'appelles? *(koh-mahn tyew tah-pel)*—"What is
your name?" or "What are you called?"

Écoute. *(ay-koot)*—Listen.

grand-mère *(grahn-mehr)*—grandmother, grandma

grand-père *(grahn-pehr)*—grandfather, grandpa

Je t'aime. *(zhuh tem)*—I love you.

la célébration *(lah say-lay-brah-syohn)*—the celebration

Les Cenelles *(leh suh-nel)*—The title of a poetry book; it refers
to a kind of berry that was prized in Louisiana.

Ma fille précieuse! *(mah feey pray-syuhz)*—My precious daughter!

ma petite *(mah puh-teet)*—my little one

madame *(mah-dahm)*—Mrs., ma'am

mademoiselle *(mahd-mwah-zel)*—Miss, young lady

magnifique *(mah-nyee-feek)*—wonderful, magnificent

maman *(mah-mahn)*—mother, mama

marchande *(mar-shahnd)*—a female seller or merchant

Mardi Gras *(mar-dee grah)*—a season of feasting and parties that lasts from January to February or March

merci *(mehr-see)*—thank you

merci beaucoup *(mehr-see boh-koo)*—thank you very much

mesdames et messieurs *(may-dahmz eh may-syuh)*—ladies and gentlemen

mon frère *(mohn frehr)*—my brother

monsieur *(muh-syuh)*—Mr., sir

monsieur le docteur *(muh-syuh luh dohk-tuhr)*—a polite way to speak to a doctor; it means something like "Sir Doctor"

non *(nohn)*—no

oui *(wee)*—yes

professeur *(proh-feh-suhr)*—teacher

Seigneur *(seh-nyuhr)*—Lord

s'il te plaît *(seel tuh pleh)*—please; if you please

tante *(tahnt)*—aunt

une minute *(ewn mee-newt)*—one minute

How to Pronounce French Names

Agnès Metoyer *(ah-nyess meh-twah-yay)*

Amie *(ah-mee)*

Antoine *(ahn-twahn)*

Armand *(ar-mahn)*

Auguste Populus *(oh-gewst poh-pew-lewss)*

Aurélia *(oh-ray-lyah)*

Belle Chénière *(bel sheh-nyehr)*

Cécé *(say-say)*

Cécile Amélie Rey *(say-seel ah-may-lee ray)*

Cochon *(koh-shohn)*

Éléonore *(ay-lay-uh-nor)*

Lejeune *(luh-zhuhn)*

Luc Rousseau *(lewk roo-soh)*

Mathilde *(mah-tild)*

Monette Bruiller *(moh-neht brew-yay)*

Océane Michel Rousseau *(oh-say-ahn mee-shel roo-soh)*

Octavia *(ohk-tah-vyah)*

Perrine Dupree *(peh-reen dew-pray)*

René *(ruh-nay)*

Villaire *(vee-layr)*

Zulime *(zew-leem)*

GET THE WHOLE STORY

Two very different girls share a unique friendship and a remarkable story. Cécile's and Marie-Grace's books take turns describing the year that changes both their lives. Read all six!

Available at bookstores and at *americangirl.com*

BOOK 1: MEET MARIE-GRACE

When Marie-Grace arrives in New Orleans, she's not sure she fits in—until an unexpected invitation opens the door to friendship.

BOOK 2: MEET CÉCILE

cc J   less

(American girls collection)

Mar   écile's
he   ever
th   safe.

BOOK 4: TROUBLES FOR CÉCILE

Yellow fever spreads through the city—and into Cécile's own home. Marie-Grace offers help, but it's up to Cécile to be strong when her family needs her most.

BOOK 5: MARIE-GRACE MAKES A DIFFERENCE

As the fever rages on, Marie-Grace and Cécile volunteer at a crowded orphanage. Then Marie-Grace discovers that it's not just the orphans who need help.

BOOK 6: CÉCILE'S GIFT

The epidemic is over, but it has changed Cécile—and New Orleans—forever. With Marie-Grace's encouragement, Cécile steps onstage to help her beloved city recover.